AS THE STORY
WAS TOLD

AS THE STORY WAS TOLD

Samuel Beckett

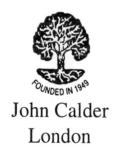

John Calder
London

As the Story Was Told (this edition) first published 1999 by
John Calder Publishers
London

The five text in this volume appeared in *Collected Shorter Prose
1945-80* in 1984 and subsequently in *As the Story Was Told* with
other texts in 1990

ISBN 0 7145 43020
Paperback

British Library Cataloguing in Publication Data
A catalogue record for this title is available from the British
Library

Printed in Canada by Webcom Ltd

AS THE
STORY WAS TOLD

As the story was told me I never went near the place during sessions. I asked what place and a tent was described at length, a small tent the colour of its surroundings. Wearying of this description I asked what sessions and these in turn were described, their object, duration, frequency and harrowing nature. I hope I was not more sensitive than the next man, but finally I had to raise my hand. I lay there quite still for a time, then asked where I was while all this was going forward. In a hut, was the answer, a small hut in a grove some two hundred yards away, a distance even the loudest cry could not carry, but must die on the way. This was not so strange as at first sight it sounded when one considered the stoutness of the canvas and the sheltered situation of the hut among the trees. Indeed the tent might have been struck where it stood and moved forward fifty yards or so without inconvenience. Lying there with closed eyes in the silence which followed this information I began to see the hut, though unlike the tent it had not been described to me, but only its situation. It reminded me strongly of a summer-house in which as a child I used to sit quite still for hours on end, on the window-seat, the whole year round. It had the same five log walls, the same coloured glass, the same diminutiveness, being not more than ten feet across and so low of ceiling that the average man could not have held himself erect in it, though of course there was no such difficulty for the child. At the centre, facing the coloured panes, stood a small upright wicker chair with arm-rests, as against the summer-house's window-seat. I sat there very straight and still, with my arms along the rests, looking out at the orange light. It must have been shortly after six, the sessions closing punctually at that hour, for as I watched a hand appeared in the doorway and held out to me a sheet of writing. I took and read it, then tore it in four and put the pieces in the waiting hand to take away. A little later the whole scene disappeared. As the story was told me the man succumbed in the end to his ill-treatment, though quite old enough at the time to die naturally of old age. I lay there a long time quite still — even as a child I was unusually still and more and more so with the passing years — till it must have seemed the story was over. But finally I asked if I knew exactly what the man — I would like to give his name but cannot — what exactly was required of the man, what it was he would not or could not say. No, was the answer, after some little hesitation no, I did not know what the poor man was required to say, in order to be pardoned, but would have recognized it at once, yes, at a glance, if I had seen it.

HEARD IN THE DARK 1

The last time you went out the snow lay on the ground. You now lying in the dark stand that morning on the sill having pulled the door gently to behind you. You lean back against the door with bowed head making ready to set out. By the time you open your eyes your feet have disappeared and the skirts of your greatcoat come to rest on the surface of the snow. The dark scene seems lit from below. You see yourself at that last outset leaning against the door with closed eyes waiting for the word from you to go. You? To be gone. Then the snowlit scene. You lie in the dark with closed eyes and see yourself there as described making ready to strike out and away across the expanse of light. You hear again the click of the door pulled gently to and the silence before the steps can start. Next thing you are on your way across the white pasture afrolic with lambs in spring and strewn with red placentae. You take the course you always take which is a beeline for the gap or ragged point in the quickset that forms the western fringe. Thither from your entering the pasture you need normally from eighteen hundred to two thousand paces depending on your humour and the state of the ground. But on this last morning many more will be necessary. Many many more. The beeline is so familiar to your feet that if necessary they could keep to it and you sightless with error on arrival of not more than a few feet north or south. And indeed without any such necessity unless from within this is what they normally do and not only here. For you advance if not with closed eyes though this as often as not at least with them fixed on the momentary ground before your feet.

That is all of nature you have seen. Since you finally bowed your head. The fleeting ground before your feet. From time to time. You do not count your steps any more. For the simple reason they number each day the same. Average day in day out the same. The way being always the same. You keep count of the days and every tenth night multiply. And add. Your father's shade is not with you any more. It fell out long ago. You do not hear your footfalls any more. Unhearing unseeing you go your way. Day after day. The same way. As if there were no other any more. For you there is no other any more. You used never to halt except to make your reckoning. So as to plod on from nought anew. This need removed as we have seen there is none in theory to halt any more. Save perhaps a moment at the outermost point. To gather yourself together for the return. And yet you do. As never before. Not for tiredness. You are no more tired now than you always were. Not because of age. You are no older now than you always were. And yet you halt as never before. So that the same hundred yards you used to cover in a matter of three to four minutes may now take you anything from fifteen to twenty. The foot falls unbidden in midstep or next for lift cleaves to the ground bringing the body to a stand. Then a speechlessness whereof the gist, Can they go on? Or better, Shall they go on? The barest gist. Stilled when finally as always hitherto they do. You lie in the dark with closed eyes and see the scene. As you could not at the time. The dark cope of sky. The dazzling land. You at a standstill in the midst. The quarterboots sunk to the tops. The skirts of the greatcoat resting on the snow. In the old bowed head in the old block hat speechless misgiving. Halfway across the pasture on your beeline to the gap. The unerring feet fast. You look behind you as you could not then and see their trail. A great swerve.

Withershins. Almost as if all at once the heart too heavy. In the end too heavy.

HEARD IN THE DARK 2

Bloom of adulthood. Try a whiff of that. On your back in the dark you remember. Ah you remember. Cloudless May day. She joins you in the little summerhouse. Entirely of logs. Both larch and fir. Six feet across. Eight from floor to vertex. Area twenty-four square feet to the furthest decimal. Two small multicoloured lights vis-à-vis. Small stained diamond panes. Under each a ledge. There on summer Sundays after his midday meal your father loved to retreat with Punch and a cushion. The waist of his trousers unbuttoned he sat on the one ledge and turned the pages. You on the other your feet dangling. When he chuckled you tried to chuckle too. When his chuckle died yours too. That you should try to imitate his chuckle pleased and amused him greatly and sometimes he would chuckle for no other reason than to hear you try to chuckle too. Sometimes you turn your head and look out through a rose-red pane. You press your little nose against the pane and all without is rosy. The years have flown and there at the same place as then you sit in the bloom of adulthood bathed in rainbow light gazing before you. She is late. You close your eyes and try to calculate the volume. Simple sums you find a help in times of trouble. A haven. You arrive in the end at seven cubic yards approximately. Even still in the timeless dark you find figures a comfort. You assume a certain heart rate and reckon how many thumps a day. A week. A month. A year. And assuming a certain lifetime a lifetime. Till the last thump. But for the moment with hardly more than seventy American billion behind you you sit in the little summerhouse working out the volume. Seven cubic yards approximately. This strikes you for some reason as improbable and you set about your sum anew. But you have not got very far when her light step is heard. Light for a woman of her size. You open with quickening pulse your eyes and a moment later that seems an eternity her face appears at the window. Mainly blue in this position the natural pallor you so admire as indeed for it no doubt wholly blue your own. For natural pallor is a property you have in common. The violet lips do not return your smile. Now this window being flush with your eyes from where you sit and the floor as near as

20

no matter with the outer ground you cannot but wonder if she has not sunk to her knees. Knowing from experience that the height or length you have in common is the sum of equal segments. For when bolt upright or lying at full stretch you cleave front to front then your knees touch and your pubes and the hairs of your heads mingle. Does it follow from this that the loss of height for the body that sits is the same as for it that kneels? At this point assuming level of seat adjustable as in the case of certain piano stools you close your eyes the better with mental measure to measure and compare the first and second segments namely from sole to kneepad and thence to pelvic girdle. How given you were both moving and at rest to the closed eye in your waking hours! By day and by night. To that perfect dark. That shadowless light. Simply to be gone. Or for affair as now. A single leg appears. Seen from above. You separate the segments and lay them side by side. It is as you half surmised. The upper is the longer and the sitter's loss the greater when seat at knee level. You leave the pieces lying there and open your eyes to find her sitting before you. All dead still. The ruby lips do not return your smile. Your gaze moves down to the breasts. You do not remember them so big. To the abdomen. Same impression. Dissolve to your father's straining against the unbuttoned waistband. Can it be she is with child without your having asked for as much as her hand? You go back into your mind. She too did you but know it has closed her eyes. So you sit face to face in the little summerhouse. With eyes closed and hands on knees. In the bloom of your adulthood. In that rainbow light. That dead still.

ONE EVENING

He was found lying on the ground. No one had missed him. No one was looking for him. An old woman found him. To put it vaguely. It happened so long ago. She was straying in search of wild flowers. Yellow only. With no eyes but for these she stumbled on him lying there. He lay face downward and arms outspread. He wore a greatcoat in spite of the time of year. Hidden by the body a long row of buttons fastened it all the way down. Buttons of all shapes and sizes. Worn upright the skirts swept the ground. That seems to hang together. Near the head a hat lay askew on the ground. At once on its brim and crown. He lay inconspicuous in the greenish coat. To catch an eye searching from afar there was only the white head. May she have seen him somewhere before? Somewhere on his feet before? Not too fast. She was all in black. The hem of her long black skirt trailed in the grass. It was close of day. Should she now move away into the east her shadow would go before. A long black shadow. It was lambing time. But there were no lambs. She could see none. Were a third party to chance that way theirs were the only bodies he would see. First that of the old woman standing. Then on drawing near it lying on the ground. That seems to hang together. The deserted fields. The old woman all in black stockstill. The body stockstill on the ground. Yellow at the end of the black arm. The white hair in the grass. The east foundering in night. Not too fast. The weather. Sky overcast all day till evening. In the west-north-west near the verge already the sun came out at last. Rain? A few drops if you will. A few drops in the morning if you will. In the present to conclude. It happened so long ago. Cooped indoors all day she comes out with the sun. She makes haste to gain the fields. Surprised to have seen no one on the way she strays feverishly in search of the wild flowers. Feverishly seeing the imminence of night. She remarks with surprise the absence of lambs in great numbers here at this time of year. She is wearing the black she took on when widowed young. It is to reflower the grave she strays in search of the flowers he had loved. But for the need of yellow at the end of the black arm there would be none. There are therefore only as few as possible. This is for her the third surprise since she came out. For they grow in plenty here at this time of year. Her old friend her shadow irks her. So much so that she turns to face the sun. Any flower wide of her course she reaches sidelong. She craves for sundown to end and to stray freely again in the long afterglow. Further to her distress the familiar rustle of her long black skirt in the grass. She moves with half-closed eyes as if drawn on into the glare. She may say to herself it is too much strangeness for a single March or April evening. No one abroad. Not a single lamb. Scarcely a flower. Shadow and rustle irksome. And to crown all the shock of her foot against a body. Chance. No one had missed him. No one was looking for him. Black and green of the garments touching now. Near the white head the yellow of the few plucked flowers. The old sunlit face. Tableau vivant if you will. In its way. All is silent from now on. For as long as she cannot move. The sun disappears at last and with it all shadow. All shadow here. Slow fade of afterglow. Night without moon or stars. All that seems to hang together. But no more about it.

NEITHER

to and fro in shadow from inner to
outershadow

from impenetrable self to impenetrable unself by way of neither

as between two lit refuges whose
doors once neared gently close, once
turned away from gently part again.

30

beckoned back and forth and turned away

heedless of the way, intent on the one gleam or the other

unheard footfalls only sound

till at last halt for good, absent for good from self and other

then no sound

then gently light unfading on that unheeded neither

unspeakable home

Written for the composer Morton Feldman, 1962

31